Texas Chili? Oh My!

Patricia Vermillion
illustrations by Kuleigh Smith

Especially for Morgan Dailey
"Happy Reading"
Patricia Vermillion
2015

TCU
PRESS

Fort Worth, Texas

Library of Congress Cataloging-in-Publication Data

Vermillion, Patricia.
 Texas chili? Oh my! / Patricia Vermillion ; illustrations by Kuleigh Smith.
     p. cm.
 Summary: Presents information about the state of Texas, its emblematic flora and fauna, and attractions.
 Includes bibliographical references.
 1. Texas--Juvenile fiction. I. Smith, Kuleigh, ill. II. Title.
 PZ7.V5917Te 2013
 [E]--dc23
                              2013013640

Text design by Rebecca A. Allen

TCU Press
TCU Box 298300
Fort Worth, Texas 76129
www.prs.tcu.edu

To order books call 1.800.826.8911

Acknowledgments

A very special thank you to Dan Williams, Melinda Esco, and Rebecca Allen for believing in my story; Katherine Folks who challenged me; my children Jennifer, Eliza, Regan, and Reagan who listened; my SCBWI group and their suggestions; Robert San Souci who inspired me to retell a traditional tale, Texas style; Robert Quackenbush for the idea of using armadillos; Pat Mattingly for her love of reading; and especially my husband John for his continued encouragement and support.

Once upon a time...

. . . deep in the south of Texas,
Mamadillo lived with her three little pups,
Bluebonnet, Mockingbird, and Sweet-Olive,
in a cozy little den!

Each day, the pups grew BIGGER and BIGGER and BIGGER.

"Little pups," grunted Mamadillo, "we are tighter than the bark on a tree. It's time to dig a den of your own."

"Now watch out for Trickster Coyote with the buttery eyes and brown baggy tail!"

"He will huff and howl and yelp and bark
till he flattens your den
and turns you into
TEXAS CHILI!"

"TEXAS CHILI? OH MY!"
grunted the little pups.

Early next morning, Mamadillo sent Bluebonnet, Mockingbird, and Sweet-Olive into the forest to dig dens of their own.

By and by,
Bluebonnet met Longhorn Lilly
carrying a load of pecan tree
branches on her big wide back.

"Howdy, Ms. Lilly," hissed
Bluebonnet.
"Those branches look strong
enough to keep out
Trickster Coyote!
May I have some of those branches
to cover my den?"

Pecan branches to cover a den? Oh my, thought Lilly.

But she gave the pup the branches anyway, and off Bluebonnet went to dig her den.

Mockingbird met Javier Javelina hauling a load of Ruby Red grapefruit on his chubby round back.

"Howdy, Mr. Javier," sang Mockingbird. "Those grapefruit look firm enough to keep out Trickster Coyote! May I have some of those grapefruits to cover my den?"

Ruby Red grapefruits to cover a den? Oh my,
thought Javier.

But he gave Mockingbird the grapefruit anyway,
and off she went to dig her den.

After a while, Sweet-Olive met Horned Toad Horace carrying a load of prickly pear cactus on his narrow thorny back.

"Howdy, Mr. Horace," hissed Sweet-Olive.
"That cactus is prickly enough to keep out Trickster Coyote!
May I have some of that cactus to cover my den?"

Prickly pear cactus to cover a den? Oh my, thought Horace.

But he gave Sweet-Olive the prickly pear cactus anyway,
and off she went to dig her den.

Down near the town of San Antonio,
there's a place called Bracken Cave,
where millions of bats live.

And somewhere near that cave,
Trickster Coyote,
with the buttery eyes and brown baggy tail,
was thinking about supper.

"I'm starving for some good old TEXAS CHILI!" he barked.

So he set out to find his key ingredient, **ARMADILLO.**

Before long,
Trickster Coyote got a whiff
of roasting pecans
and **ONE** armadillo!

His long hairy nose sniffed
its way to Bluebonnet's den
covered with pecan branches.

"Little armadillo, let me in!" howled Trickster Coyote.

"No, no, no," grunted Bluebonnet. "Not by the rings on my skinny, skin, skin!"

"Then I'll huff and I'll howl and I'll yelp and I'll bark till I flatten your den!"

So while Trickster Coyote was busy huffing and howling and yelping and barking, Bluebonnet ran out her back door right over to Mockingbird's den.

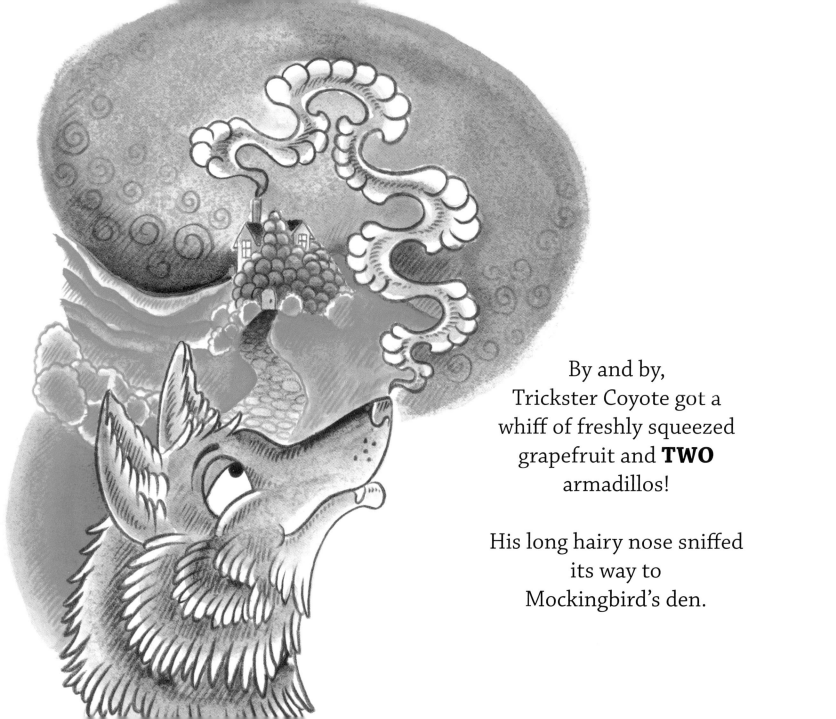

By and by,
Trickster Coyote got a
whiff of freshly squeezed
grapefruit and **TWO**
armadillos!

His long hairy nose sniffed
its way to
Mockingbird's den.

"Little armadillos, let me in!"
howled Trickster Coyote.

"No, no, no," grunted
Bluebonnet and
Mockingbird.
"Not by the rings on our
skinny, skin, skin!"

"Then I'll huff and I'll howl
and I'll yelp and I'll bark till I
flatten your den!"

So while Trickster Coyote was huffing and howling and yelping and barking, Bluebonnet and Mockingbird ran out the back door right on over to Sweet-Olive's den.

Later on in the day,
as the sun was setting in the golden Texas sky,
Trickster Coyote got a whiff of the
fragrant cactus flower and
THREE armadillos!

His long hairy nose sniffed its way to
Sweet-Olive's den.

"Little armadillos, let me in!"
howled Trickster Coyote.

"No, no, no!" grunted Sweet-Olive, Mockingbird,
and Bluebonnet.
"Not by the rings on our skinny, skin, skin!"

"Then I'll huff and I'll howl and I'll yelp and I'll
bark till I flatten your den!"

So Trickster Coyote huffed and he howled and he
yelped and he barked and he even swung
his baggy brown tail,
but he could not flatten that den.

By this time Trickster Coyote
was breathing mighty heavy.
His tail was throbbing,
but he was determined to have
TEXAS CHILI
for supper.

He jumped on the
roof of the cactus den and yelled,
"I'm coming down
this chimney to fix me some
TEXAS CHILI!"

Quick as a wink,
Trickster Coyote jumped down that chimney,
tail and paws covered with thorns.
He plopped right smack into a boiling pot of
fire ants that Sweet-Olive had
cooked up for supper.

Trickster Coyote's buttery eyes turned blood red as soon as those
boiling ants got ahold of him!
Why, he was a' huffing and a' howling and a' yelping and a' barking and a' wiggling
his brown baggy tail right out of that pot!

"Ye doggies! Giddy-up! My tail's on fire!"
howled Trickster Coyote.

Bluebonnet, Mockingbird, and Sweet-Olive
sat down to a delicious supper of spicy fire ant tacos
with prickly pear cactus salsa, and for dessert,
vanilla ice cream topped with
sugar-roasted pecans.

The young pups would be safe for a while. They raised their mugs of Ruby Red grapefruit juice and made a toast.

"Mamadillo would be so proud!"

And that, my friends, is the end of this story.
But watch out for Trickster Coyote
with the blood-red eyes and
the brown baggy tail!

If you aren't careful,
he just might turn you into
TEXAS CHILI!

the end.

Glossary of Texas Terms

Bluebonnet: the Texas state flower with spikes of blue petals. In Texas, they bloom from early March to the end of May.

Bracken Cave: a cave outside of San Antonio where over twenty million bats live. More bats live here than anywhere else in the world!

Chili: a spicy stew made with peppers and meat. The name is short for *chile con carne*, which is Spanish for chile pepper with meat.

Coyote: a small, dog-like mammal with large ears and a long nose; often a trickster in folklore. These animals are also known as prairie wolves.

Den: a wild animal's home.

Fire Ant: an insect that lives in a colony with a queen and her workers. They have a stinging bite!

Javelina: a small wild hog with a black and gray coat.

Mockingbird: the Texas state bird that copies the songs and sounds of other creatures.

Nine-banded armadillo: a small mammal with a bony plate covering and strong claws. It is the only mammal known to eat fire ants. They are omnivores, meaning they eat both animals and plants. Armadillo babies are called pups.

Olive branch: a symbol of peace found on the state seal of Texas.

Pecan tree: the Texas state tree that produces the delicious pecan nut.

Prickly pear cactus: the Texas state plant with leafless spiny stems and flowers that can be eaten.

Ruby Red grapefruit: the Texas state fruit grown in Texas for over one hundred years.

Texas horned toad: the Texas state reptile, which feeds on ants and a few other insects. Although they are commonly called toads or frogs, they are actually lizards. Horned toads shoot blood from their eyes when frightened.

Texas longhorn: a breed of cattle with a horn span of seven feet.

Objectives for Student Learning

1. Students will make predictions about the story using words, illustrations, and the title.
2. Students will identify picture details.
3. Students will describe the elements of a fairy tale and folktale.
4. Students will compare and contrast *Texas Chili* to the original folktale of the *Three Little Pigs*.
5. Students will identify important details such as who, what, when, where, and why that relate to the author's purpose.
6. Students will identify the characters, objects, actions, and settings that relate to Texas.
7. Students will identify the beginning, middle, and end of the story.
8. Students will identify Texas symbols.

Bibliography

Jango-Cohen, Judith. *Digging Armadillos.* Minneapolis, MN: Lerner, 1999.

Lanier, Wendy. *The Pebble First Guide to Texas Symbols.* North Mankato, MN: Capstone, 2009.

Lineberger, Dan. "Aggie Horticulture." *Aggie Horticulture Network.* http://aggie-horticulture.tamu.edu.

McAuliffe, Emily. *Texas Facts and Symbols.* New York: Scholastic Library, 1998.

Chris Ward's Texas Chili

(Even Trickster Coyote would love this one!)

Ready in: 2.5 hours
Servings: 20

3 tablespoons bacon drippings
2 large onions, chopped
8 pounds beef stew meat or coarse ground beef
5 cloves garlic, finely chopped
4 tablespoons ground red chile pepper
4 tablespoons mild chili powder
1 tablespoon ground cumin
1/4 cup sweet Hungarian paprika

1 teaspoon dried Mexican oregano
3-10 oz. cans tomato sauce
1-6 oz. can tomato paste
3 cups water
2 tablespoons salt
1/4 cup dried parsley (optional)
1 fresh jalapeño pepper
1 cup masa harina flour

1. Melt the bacon drippings in a large heavy pot over medium heat. Add the onions and cook until they are translucent.
2. Combine the beef with the garlic, ground chile, chili powder, and cumin. Add this meat and spice combination to the onions in the pot. Break up any meat that sticks together as you cook, stirring occasionally, about 30 minues, until meat is evenly browned. Sprinkle in paprika and oregano.
3. Pour in the tomato sauce, tomato paste, water, salt, parsley, and jalapeño. Bring to a boil, lower heat, and simmer, uncovered, for 1 hour. (**Note**: True Texans *do not* add beans to their chili, but you can add as many cans of drained and rinsed pinto beans as you wish.)
4. As the jalapeño softens during cooking, squeeze it against the sides of the pot to release more heat if desired.
5. Mix in the masa harina and cook while stirring for 30 minutes longer, or until desired consistency is achieved. Taste and adjust seasonings.

From the kitchen of the Mercury in Dallas, Texas

About the Author

Patricia Vermillion serves as the librarian at the Lamplighter School in Dallas, Texas. She has written articles for *Mississippi Magazine, School Library Monthly*, and *Library Sparks Magazine*. This is her first picture book. She is married to a TCU alumnus and has a passion for **PURPLE**.

About the Illustrator

Kuleigh Smith attended the Art Institute in Dallas and served as director of the Galeria Sin Fronteras (a gallery without borders). He built guitars with Bill Collings and is an avid fan of classic cars and bikes. He resides in Austin with his wife and daughter.